I scream, you scream,
we all scream . . . for cake?

Tory looked down at the cake. She made a face. "This better be *all* chocolate. I hate that icky jelly stuff!"

"I'm sure it's everything you wished for, dear," her mother said.

Nancy watched as Harriet cut the cake. Suddenly Tory let out a piercing scream. Green slime spurted out of the cake along with rubber creepy crawlies and fake eyeballs!

A glob of slime hit Tory in the face with a splat. A rubber worm stuck to her hair and dangled over her nose.

"Eeeewwwww!" Tory cried.

The Nancy Drew Notebooks

Available from MINSTREL Books

THE
NANCY DREW
NOTEBOOKS®

#27

Trouble Takes the Cake

CAROLYN KEENE
ILLUSTRATED BY ANTHONY ACCARDO

A MINSTREL® BOOK

Published by POCKET BOOKS
New York   London   Toronto   Sydney   Tokyo   Singapore

A MINSTREL PAPERBACK *Original*

 A Minstrel Book published by
POCKET BOOKS, a division of Simon & Schuster Inc.
1230 Avenue of the Americas, New York, NY 10020

Copyright © 1998 by Simon & Schuster Inc.

ISBN: 0-671-02141-9

First Minstrel Books printing November 1998

10 9 8 7 6 5 4 3 2 1

NANCY DREW, THE NANCY DREW NOTEBOOKS, A MINSTREL BOOK and colophon are registered trademarks of Simon & Schuster Inc.

Cover art by Joanie Schwarz

Printed in the U.S.A.

1

Boo Burgers and Franken-furters

Is Keller's really the biggest department store in the world, Aunt Eloise?" eight-year-old Nancy Drew asked as they walked through the spinning doors.

"Bigger than the one in River Heights?" Nancy's best friend Bess Marvin asked.

"See for yourself, girls," Aunt Eloise said when they were inside the store.

"Awesome!" Nancy cried. She pushed back her reddish blond bangs so she could see everything.

The store was filled with shoppers. Rows of counters were covered with makeup, handbags, and colorful gloves. There was even a man playing a piano under a huge chandelier.

Nancy's other best friend, George Fayne, whistled. "This store makes the one back home look like a lemonade stand!"

Nancy couldn't have been more excited. Her aunt Eloise Drew had invited her, Bess, and George to New York City to spend a three-day holiday weekend.

Aunt Eloise rubbed her hands together. "Let's shop till we drop, girls!" she said.

"Your aunt is so cool," Bess whispered to Nancy as they walked through the crowd.

"And she's a *teacher*," Nancy added. "Can you imagine her class trips?"

George stopped walking. She wrinkled her nose. "What's that stinky smell?"

Nancy saw that they were passing a row of perfume counters. "It must be all the perfume," she said.

A woman in a black dress stepped in front of them with a small glass bottle.

"Hello! Would you care to try Beautiful Blooms?" she asked.

George jumped behind Nancy. "Yuck! Don't let her squirt me with that stuff."

Bess held out her wrist. "I'd like to try some, please," she said.

Nancy laughed. Bess and George were cousins, but they were totally different.

Aunt Eloise tried the perfume, too. Then they rode the escalator to the toy department on the seventh floor.

"I've never seen so many toys!" Nancy said. She gazed at shelves filled with games, dolls, and stuffed animals.

"I'm going to buy some art supplies for my class," Aunt Eloise said. "Stick close together and don't wander off."

Nancy and her friends nodded. Then they stared at the toys.

"I want to check out the sports equipment," George said.

"A pink bicycle!" Bess cried. Her blond ponytail bounced as she ran to it.

Nancy walked around slowly.

I want something that will remind me of my trip to New York, she thought.

Then she saw it. Her favorite fashion doll stood on a shelf, dressed as the Statue of Liberty. The doll wore a flowing green gown and the famous Miss Liberty crown.

"It's perfect," Nancy whispered. She picked it up carefully.

But just as she was about to show it to Bess and George, she felt someone yank it out of her hands.

"It's *mine!*" said an angry voice.

Nancy looked up. A girl with curly brown hair clutched the doll to her chest. She wore a red coat and matching hat.

"What do you mean it's *yours?*" Nancy asked as Bess and George ran over.

The girl stuck her freckled chin in the air. "My mother said I could have

anything I want today. And I want *this!*"

"Give me a break," George mumbled.

Nancy sighed. "If you want it that badly, then take it," she told the girl.

"Now, why don't you be like Little Bo Peep's sheep and *get lost!*" George said.

"Very funny. Ha. Ha," the girl muttered. Then she huffed off.

"Why did you let her have the doll, Nancy?" Bess asked. "It was the only one."

Nancy shrugged. "I don't want to spoil my trip to New York City by fighting with a snooty-nosed brat."

"Oh, well," George said. "At least you'll never see *her* again."

Instead of the doll, Nancy bought a stuffed bear wearing a New York City T-shirt. George bought a soccer ball keychain. Bess bought a plastic bracelet.

"I hope shopping gave you a big appetite," Aunt Eloise said. "Because our next stop is Haunted Harriet's."

"Haunted Harriet's?" Nancy asked.

"It's a restaurant, and the theme is a haunted house," Aunt Eloise explained.

"Uh-oh," Bess said. "Sounds spooky."

"Don't worry," Aunt Eloise said. "Harriet is a good friend of mine. We were roommates in college."

"What was she like?" Nancy asked.

"Harriet always loved spooky movies and costumes," Aunt Eloise said. "She once slipped a rubber spider under my pillow."

"Neat!" George cried.

"I think you'll like Haunted Harriet's," Aunt Eloise said. "They have great Boo Burgers and Frankenfurters."

Aunt Eloise hailed a taxi. They piled in and rode down a street called Broadway.

"There are so many people in New York," Bess said as they stared out the window. "Can you imagine solving a mystery here, Nancy?"

Nancy smiled. She was the best detective at Carl Sandburg Elementary

School. She even had a blue detective notebook where she wrote down her clues.

"Nope," Nancy said. "But I brought my detective notebook just in case."

The taxi stopped in front of a building wrapped in cobwebs. Aunt Eloise paid the driver, and they went inside.

Nancy's eyes sparkled. "This place *does* look like a haunted house," she said.

"The waiters and waitresses are dressed like monsters!" George exclaimed.

A man dressed as the Hunchback of Notre Dame limped over. "I have a *hunch* you're the Drew party. Follow me to the dessert kitchen."

The girls giggled as the hunchback led them into a bright kitchen. A woman with black hair came out from behind a counter.

"Eloise!" the woman cried. She ran over and gave Nancy's aunt a hug.

"Hi, Harriet," Eloise Drew said. "I'd like you to meet my niece, Nancy."

"Hello," Nancy said. "These are my best friends, Bess and George."

"Welcome, girls," Harriet said.

"Do you own the restaurant *and* bake, too?" George asked Harriet.

"Yes, but I have help," Harriet said. She walked over to a young man standing by the oven. "Meet my assistant, Scott. He just graduated from cooking school."

Scott waved shyly. Nancy noticed a large pocket on the front of his apron. It was filled with shiny baking tools.

"Scott is such a good baker, he has his own cabinet," Harriet said. She pointed to a cupboard with Scott's name on it.

Nancy looked around and saw a table filled with chocolate cakes. "Those cakes look yummy, Harriet," she said.

"One of the cakes is going to a special birthday girl," Harriet said.

"Which cake?" Nancy asked.

"Why don't you choose?" Harriet asked.

Nancy knew which cake to pick.

9

"That one," she said, pointing to the fourth cake. "The one with the pretty pink roses."

Harriet picked up the cake. "I'll put candles on it right now," she said.

"Who is the birthday girl, Harriet?" George asked.

"Just look out the door," Harriet suggested. "She's sitting with her mom next to the mummy's tomb."

The girls ran to the kitchen door and peeked out. Then Nancy groaned.

"What's wrong, Nancy?" Bess asked.

Nancy wrinkled her nose. "It's the snooty girl from Keller's Department Store!"

2

Happy Birthday to Goo!

Are you sure it's her?" Bess asked.

Nancy nodded. "It's her, all right."

George made a face. "She even looks snooty from way back here."

Nancy turned to Harriet. "What makes her so special?" she asked.

"Her name is Tory Buckingham, and her mom is a reporter for *Big Apple* magazine," Harriet explained. "If Mrs. Buckingham likes Haunted Harriet's, she might give it a great review."

"How can she not like this place?" Nancy asked. "It's super!"

"Thanks," Harriet said with a grin. "Now, how about a *super* lunch?"

The hunchback led the girls and

Aunt Eloise to a table under a giant spiderweb. Nancy was happy to see that the snooty girl was on the other side of the dining area.

"Ohmygosh!" Bess whispered after they sat down. "Look what's coming!"

Nancy saw a young woman wearing a black-and-silver fright wig. Her face was green, and her gown was tattered.

The creepy woman came over and opened her mouth. Inside were white, gleaming fangs. "Care for a bite?" she asked.

"Nope." George giggled. "But *fangs* anyway!"

"I am the Bride of Frankenstein," the woman said. She leaned over and winked. "But you can call me Sally. Have you decided what to order?"

Nancy nodded. "I'll have the Yummy Mummy Casserole," she said.

"And I'll have the Godzilla Gardenburger," Aunt Eloise said.

George looked up at Sally. "Are the Wolfman Waffles good?" she asked.

"Are you kidding?" Sally laughed. "They're a *howl!*"

Bess ordered a Boo Burger with Monster-Mash Potatoes. Sally wrote down their orders, then walked over to the next table.

"Can we look around the restaurant now, Aunt Eloise?" Nancy asked.

"Sure," Aunt Eloise said. "As long as you come back to the table in ten minutes."

"We will," Nancy promised.

But just as the girls stood up from their seats, they heard a loud crash.

"What was that?" Nancy asked. She spun around and saw Sally kneeling over a pile of broken dishes. There was gooey chocolate syrup all over the floor.

"Sally dropped a tray at the next table," George whispered.

Nancy saw Harriet rush out of the kitchen. She did not look happy.

"Sally, this has got to stop," Harriet said. "Yesterday you dropped a whole Coconut Scream Pie!"

"It won't happen again, Harriet," Sally promised.

"That's what you say every day." Harriet sighed. She shook her head and went back to the dessert kitchen.

As the girls carefully stepped around the broken mess, Nancy heard Sally mumbling to herself.

"Harriet is always yelling at me," she was saying. "I can't take it anymore!"

Nancy, Bess, and George forgot about the accident as they explored Haunted Harriet's. There were surprises everywhere.

A hairy werewolf played an old-fashioned piano. "Blue moooooon!" he sang.

Not far from the werewolf was a mad scientist with wild blue hair.

"Welcome to my lab," the mad scientist said. She waved her hand over a row of beakers. They bubbled with green slime.

"What makes the slime bubble?" George asked.

"Glad you asked," the mad scientist

said. She picked up a brown bottle and popped off the lid. Green gook oozed out from the top.

Bess jumped back. "Eew!" she cried.

"It's my secret formula!" the mad scientist cried. "And it's alive! It's alive!"

Just then Nancy felt someone breathing on the back of her neck. She whirled around and shrieked. Right behind her was a vampire!

"Good afternoon," the vampire said with a strange accent. He smiled to show a mouth filled with pointy fangs.

"G-g-good afternoon," Nancy stammered.

The vampire's face was as white as chalk. His lips were dark red. He wore a flowing black cape.

"Allow me to introduce myself," the vampire said. "I am Count Snackula!"

The count pulled a silver tray from under his cape. On it were candy bats in different flavors. "Care for a snack?"

Nancy was relieved. The vampire was funny, not scary.

"Are they good?" Bess asked.

Count Snackula nodded. "You can *count* on it," he said.

After the girls picked their favorite flavors, Count Snackula disappeared behind a heavy, black curtain.

"Where did he go?" George asked.

Nancy pointed to a sign over the curtain. It read: Count Snackula's Castle.

"It's probably part of the joke," Nancy said. "Let's look inside."

The girls peeked through the curtain. The room was dark, but Nancy could see Count Snackula. He was talking to another monster with a white wig and a tall black hat.

Nancy strained her ears to listen.

Count Snackula groaned. "Being Count Snackula bites, Bruce."

"Why?" the other monster asked.

"I hate these stupid fangs!" Count Snackula cried. "And if Harriet wants someone to hand out candy, why doesn't she get Willy Wonka?"

"Wow," Nancy whispered to Bess

17

and George. "He's not a happy camper."

"You think I like being Phantom of the Omelets?" the other monster asked. He picked up a basket of eggs. "How many times can I say, 'Try the omelets. They're *egg*-cellent'?"

"But I *loved* being the mad scientist," Count Snackula said. "Until Harriet gave the part to someone else."

The Phantom of the Omelets sighed. "Nobody handled slime the way you did."

Count Snackula paced back and forth. "Soon Harriet will regret it," he said.

"Regret it?" the Phantom asked.

Count Snackula rubbed his white hands together. "When she gets the cake. Mwah-hah-hah-haaaaaa!"

The count whipped his cape and spun around. The girls ducked outside the curtain just in time.

"Did he see us?" Bess asked as they ran away from Count Snackula's Castle.

"I don't think so," Nancy said. "But let's go back to our table."

"Good idea," George said. "That was too creepy, even for me."

The girls made their way through the dining area. But just as they got close to their table, the lights went out!

"Now what's going on?" Nancy asked.

Just then Nancy saw the doors to the dessert kitchen swing open. Harriet marched out carrying a birthday cake with glowing candles. Scott followed.

"Happy birthday to yoooou!" Harriet and Scott sang.

"That's the cake you picked, Nancy," Bess said.

"Too bad it's going to that snooty girl, Tory," George grumbled.

Nancy smiled. She loved birthday cakes. "Let's watch her blow out the candles," she suggested.

Nancy, Bess, and George ran closer to Tory's table. The lights flashed back on just as Harriet placed the cake in front of Tory.

Tory looked down at the cake. She made a face. "This better be *all* chocolate. I hate that icky jelly stuff!"

"I'm sure it's everything you wished for, dear," her mother said.

Nancy watched as Harriet cut the cake. Suddenly Tory let out a piercing scream. Green slime spurted out of the cake along with rubber creepy crawlies and fake eyeballs!

A glob of slime hit Tory in the face with a splat. A rubber worm stuck to her hair and dangled over her nose.

"Eeeewww!" Tory cried. "Eeeewww!"

3

Things Get Hairy

Is this part of the show?" a little boy called from another table.

Tory's mother jumped up from her chair. A fake eyeball rolled off her lap.

"What is the meaning of this?" she demanded.

George giggled. "Tory looks pretty gory," she whispered.

"I have no idea how this happened," Harriet insisted. She turned to Scott. He quickly shrugged.

"Will the person who did this horrible trick please step forward?" Harriet called out.

The monster-waiters shrugged and shook their heads.

Then Tory jumped up from her chair and marched over to Nancy.

"I know you!" Tory shouted. She pointed a dripping, slimy green finger at Nancy. "You were that nasty girl in the department store!"

Harriet walked over and put her arm around Nancy's shoulder.

"This is Nancy Drew," Harriet said. "She's a very nice girl and a good friend of mine."

"Ah-ha!" Tory shouted in Nancy's face. "If you're a friend of Harriet's, then you probably helped her bake that gross cake!"

Bess marched over to Tory. "Nancy didn't bake it. She just picked it."

"Bess!" Nancy cried.

"Picked it?" Tory screamed. She turned to her mother. "See? She *was* part of it!"

Nancy turned around. All the people in the restaurant were staring at her. She could see her aunt Eloise walking over.

"But I—" Nancy started to say.

Tory's mother turned to Harriet. "If you think I'm going to write nice things about this terrible place, forget it."

"But, Mrs. Buckingham—" Harriet pleaded.

Mrs. Buckingham grabbed Tory's slimy hand. "We're going," she said coldly.

Tory stuck her tongue out at Nancy as she stormed off with her mother.

"I didn't have anything to do with that cake," Nancy insisted.

"We know you didn't, Nancy," Aunt Eloise said.

Bess grabbed Nancy's arm. "This is a real mystery, Nancy. Why don't you try to solve it?" she asked.

"Yeah, Nancy," George said. "You *did* bring your notebook, right?"

"Yes," Nancy said. "But this isn't River Heights. It's New York City, the biggest city in the world."

"So what?" Bess said. "You're the best detective in the world."

Nancy gave it a thought. Then she reached into her pocket and pulled out her blue detective notebook. "Okay," she said. "I'll give it a try."

"Way to go, Nancy!" George said.

"We knew you'd do it!" Bess cheered.

Nancy turned to Harriet. "I'd like to help you find the person who played that terrible trick."

"Harriet, I don't think I ever told you that my niece solves mysteries," Aunt Eloise said.

Harriet shrugged. "No. But what's one more surprise?" she asked.

The busboys hurried to clean up the slimy mess.

"Can we come back here tomorrow to look for clues?" Nancy asked Harriet and Aunt Eloise.

Harriet nodded. "I could really use your help in getting to the bottom of this," she said.

"And I have some math tests to grade tomorrow," Aunt Eloise said. "So it's fine with me, too."

"Thanks, Aunt Eloise," Nancy said.

"I'll bring you girls to the restaurant

tomorrow morning as soon as it opens," Aunt Eloise said.

"Now, why don't you all sit down and eat your lunch?" Harriet said. "I promise it won't be filled with spiders or worms."

"Gross!" Nancy laughed.

The food was delicious, but Nancy was still hungry to solve the case.

"I want to start writing a list of suspects tonight," Nancy said.

"I think the biggest suspect is Count Snackula," George said. "Remember what he said about getting even with some cake?"

"And that other monster said the count had a way with slime," Bess added.

"I know," Nancy said. She wiped her mouth with her napkin. "But as my dad says, everyone is innocent until proven guilty."

Carson Drew was a lawyer and often helped Nancy with her cases.

"Don't plan to work too much tonight," Aunt Eloise said. "Because we're going to the top of the Empire State Building."

Nancy gasped. "That's one of the tallest buildings in the world!"

"And King Kong climbed it in the movies," George added.

"Uh-oh," Bess said. "I'm afraid of heights and giant gorillas."

"What *aren't* you afraid of, Bess?" George asked.

Aunt Eloise put her napkin on the table. "If everyone is finished, I'd like to say goodbye to Harriet."

They went inside the dessert kitchen. Scott wasn't there, but Harriet was busy rolling out cookie dough.

While Aunt Eloise spoke to Harriet, Nancy looked around the kitchen for clues. Suddenly she saw something.

"Bess, George!" Nancy called.

"What's up?" George asked as she and Bess ran over.

Nancy pointed to the white tiled floor. "Look at those weird footprints."

There were three footprints near the oven. One was clearer than the others.

George tilted her head. "They're weird, all right," she said slowly.

Bess stepped back and gulped. "They don't even look human!"

4

A Message to Nancy

Those footprints look like some kind
of paws," Nancy said. She pointed to
one of the prints. It had a few hairs
stuck on top. "Fuzzy paws!"

George glanced over at Harriet.
"Harriet has normal feet," she
whispered.

"So did Scott," Bess said. "I think."

"Most of the people here wear costumes, remember?" Nancy asked.

"Oh, yeah," George said.

"And the cakes come out of this
oven," Nancy said. "So if the footprints
are near the oven—"

"Then a hairy-footed monster might
have baked the creepy cake," Bess said.

Nancy took her notebook out of her pocket. On a fresh page she wrote, "Mystery at Haunted Harriet's." Under that she wrote, "Clues." And under that she wrote, "Fuzzy Pawprints." Then she turned the page and wrote, "Suspects."

"I'm going to make a list of all the monsters who have hairy feet," Nancy said. "Starting with King Kong."

"Don't forget Bigfoot," Bess said.

"Or Jason Hutchings," George said, laughing.

Jason was a bratty boy in their third-grade class.

"Jason's feet aren't hairy," Bess joked. "Just smelly."

"Eew!" Nancy laughed. Then her eyes lit up. "Hey, I know!"

"What?" Bess asked.

"The werewolf!" Nancy said. "He had hairy claws *and* paws."

"Should we tell Harriet and your aunt Eloise?" Bess asked.

"Not yet," Nancy said. "I want to look for more clues first."

Aunt Eloise gave the girls permission to walk around the restaurant again.

"Harriet?" Nancy asked as she and her friends were leaving the kitchen. "Does the werewolf ever come in here?"

"The werewolf?" Harriet repeated. She shook her head. "No. I don't allow hairy costumes in the kitchen."

Ah-ha! Nancy thought. If the werewolf isn't allowed in the kitchen, then he *was* doing something sneaky!

The girls ran straight to the piano. But the werewolf was gone.

"Do you know where the werewolf went?" Nancy asked the Hunchback of Notre Dame.

"No," the hunchback said. "But perhaps he's moonlighting. Mwah! Hah! Hah!"

Nancy laughed and rolled her eyes.

"But seriously, folks," the hunchback said. "I did see the werewolf go downstairs to the basement."

"Thanks," Nancy said as the hunchback limped away. She walked up to the piano and carefully pressed a key.

Then she saw something that made her jaw drop.

"Bess! George!" Nancy said. "There's chocolate all over these piano keys. Do you know what that means?"

George shrugged. "That the werewolf's a slob?" she asked.

"No," Nancy said. "It means the werewolf might have baked the creepy chocolate cake."

"Are you going to question the werewolf, Nancy?" Bess asked.

Nancy nodded. "Let's go down to the basement right now," she said.

The girls searched until they found a staircase leading downstairs.

"I don't want to go down there," Bess said. "It looks scary."

But Nancy and George were already halfway down.

"Wait for meeee!" Bess called.

At the bottom of the stairs was a big room. It was filled with dusty, spooky-looking things.

"Look at those portraits against the

wall," George said. "The eyes look as if they're moving."

"Quit it!" Bess squealed.

"And look at that giant fake spider hanging from the ceiling," Nancy said.

George wiggled her fingers. "How do you know it's fake?" she whispered.

"I said, cut it out!" Bess wailed.

The girls walked between mummy tombs and large stuffed grizzly bears. Just then Nancy heard a strange smacking noise. She felt her skin crawl.

"Did you hear that?" Nancy whispered.

Smack-smack!

Bess and George nodded.

Nancy slowly followed the noise.

Smack-smack-smack!

"It sounds as if it's coming from there," Nancy said. She pointed toward a row of gray tombstones.

Smack-smack-smack!

"That one," George whispered. She pointed to a tombstone that read: Violet Veggie. Rest in Peas.

"I'm checking it out," Nancy said.

She moved slowly to the tombstone. But just as she was about to walk around it, something big and hairy popped up from behind!

"Eeeek!" the girls screamed.

Nancy covered her face with her hands.

"Hey! What's up?" the creature said.

Nancy peeked out from between her fingers. It was the werewolf. And he had chocolate all over the gloves of his fuzzy costume.

"What are *you* doing here?" Nancy asked. She stared at the smudged paws.

The werewolf looked down at his paws and sighed. "Okay, okay. You caught me wolfing down the evidence."

"Did you say evidence?" Nancy gasped.

The werewolf gave a big sigh. Then he pointed behind the tombstone. Nancy looked down and saw a pile of half-eaten chocolate brownies lying on a napkin.

"I sneaked these brownies out of the dessert kitchen," the werewolf confessed.

"Why?" Nancy asked.

"I have this craving for anything sweet," the werewolf explained. "So I've been secretly snatching desserts. Strawberry tarts, lemon squares, chocolate eclairs. Anything I can get my paws on."

"But you're not allowed in the kitchen," Bess said. "You're too hairy."

The werewolf nodded. "I always wait until Harriet and Scott are out of the kitchen. Today I sneaked in while they were giving the birthday cake to that girl."

"Do you know anything about that creepy cake?" Nancy asked.

The werewolf shook his head. "Only that it was a big shame. How can anyone ruin a delicious chocolate cake like that?"

Nancy decided that the werewolf was no longer a suspect. He was just a hairy guy with a big sweet tooth.

"What you did was wrong, too," Nancy told the werewolf.

"I know, I know," the werewolf said. Then his eyes looked frightened behind his fuzzy mask. "You girls aren't going to tell Harriet, are you?"

"Not if you promise never to do it again," Nancy said.

"It's a deal," the werewolf said. "As soon as I finish these brownies, I'm going to be a new wolf-man!" He held out his furry paw to shake. Nancy jumped back. It was full of sticky chocolate.

"Whoops," the werewolf said.

As the girls walked toward the staircase, Nancy noticed a row of lockers against the wall. One had the name *Sally* written on it.

"We'd better go back to your aunt, Nancy," George said. "She's probably waiting for us."

"You're right," Nancy agreed.

The girls climbed the staircase. Then they walked through a long hall with mirrors on the wall.

George stopped to look into a mirror.

"Hey, that's not my reflection." She laughed. "It's some dog's!"

Nancy looked over George's shoulder. "That's a hologram. It makes flat pictures look real."

Bess giggled as she looked into the next mirror. "My face looks like stretchy taffy," she said. Then she looked worried. "I don't really look like this, do I?"

"No way!" Nancy laughed. But when she looked into the next mirror, she stopped laughing.

Smeared on the glass in green slime were the words "Nancy, go home!"

Nancy felt a shiver down her back.

"Uh-oh," she said. "I think this means me!"

5

Clues and Boos

What a horrible message," Bess said.

Nancy stared at the green gook dripping down the mirror. "It looks like the slime that was in the creepy cake."

George ran her fingers through her dark curls. "So?" she asked.

"So the person who wrote this message might be the same person who baked the cake," Nancy said. "Who else would want me to go home?"

Nancy took out her notebook and copied the message. Then she, Bess, and George went to join Aunt Eloise.

They went straight to Aunt Eloise's apartment to freshen up. Then they took a bus to the Empire State Building.

"This is the longest elevator ride I've ever taken," George said on their way up to the top.

"Don't remind me!" Bess groaned.

When they reached the top, Nancy couldn't believe her eyes. The observation deck wound all the way around the building. They could see a different part of New York City from each side.

"Wow!" Bess said. "It's too pretty up here to be afraid of heights."

Nancy agreed with Bess. The lights of the city twinkled all around them.

"New York is even bigger than I thought," Nancy said.

"You bet," Aunt Eloise said. "There are five boroughs—Manhattan, Brooklyn, Queens, the Bronx, and Staten Island."

"I can see three bridges from here," George said.

"You can even see the state of New Jersey across the Hudson River," Aunt Eloise said.

Nancy stared out at the sights.

Somewhere out there is the baker of

the creepy cake, she thought. And I'm going to find him or her.

It got chilly, so the girls and Aunt Eloise went inside to the snack bar.

Nancy, Bess, and George sat at a table while Aunt Eloise paid for the snacks.

"Okay. Let's get to work," Nancy said. She opened her notebook and crossed the werewolf's name from her list of suspects.

"What other suspects do you have, Nancy?" Bess asked.

George jabbed at the notebook. "Write down Count Snackula. He seems guilty to me."

Nancy wrote the count's name in her notebook. "He's a good suspect, but we still need more proof," she said.

"Who else, Nancy?" Bess asked.

Nancy twirled her pen between her fingers. "How about Sally?" she asked.

"Sally?" George asked. "You mean our waitress?"

Nancy nodded. "Remember when

Sally dropped that whole tray of chocolate sundaes?" she asked.

Bess groaned. "How can we forget?"

"Well, Sally was mad at Harriet for always yelling at her," Nancy said.

"Maybe she was mad enough to ruin Tory's birthday cake," George said. "So her mother would write bad things about Haunted Harriet's in her magazine."

Nancy nodded. "I also saw Sally's locker in the basement today. If she did bake the cake, then her locker might be full of all sorts of clues."

"Like leftover slime and rubber creepy crawlies," George said. "And gushy fake eyeballs."

Nancy tapped her fingers on the table. "We can't look *inside* Sally's locker tomorrow, but we *can* look around it."

Aunt Eloise brought over a tray of hot chocolate and cookies. When they finished eating, they rode the elevator down.

"That was neat," George said. "What are we going to see now?"

Bess yawned. "How about our beds? I'm sleepy."

"You girls did have a busy day today," Aunt Eloise said.

And it's going to be even busier tomorrow, Nancy thought. We've got a mystery to solve!

Sunday morning couldn't come fast enough for Nancy. After a yummy breakfast of bagels and cream cheese, Eloise took all three girls to Haunted Harriet's.

"Maybe we can have Boo Burgers later for lunch," Bess said as they followed the hunchback to the dessert kitchen.

"We're here to work, Bess," Nancy said. "Besides, we just had breakfast."

When they reached the kitchen, Harriet was there to greet them.

"You can investigate the restaurant as long as you check in with me every half hour," Harriet said.

43

"We will," Nancy promised. Just then she smelled something funny.

Harriet must have smelled it, too, because she wrinkled her nose. "The muffins!" she cried.

Scott ran to the oven and opened it. He pulled out a huge tray of black, crusty muffins.

"Scott, you burned our only batch of Monster Muffins," Harriet said. "That's not like you."

"S-s-sorry," Scott said.

Nancy felt bad for Scott.

"Let's go," she whispered to Bess and George.

They headed for the staircase leading to the basement. Sticking close together, they went downstairs.

"Yuck!" Bess whispered as she stepped on a rubber rat. "This place is so creepy!"

"The lockers are over there," Nancy said. She pointed to a row of metal lockers against one of the walls.

The girls walked over to Sally's locker. There was no lock on the door.

"It's open!" Nancy said excitedly.

"Go for it, Nancy," George whispered.

Nancy yanked the door open. Then she looked inside and gasped. There was something inside the locker— something wrapped in tattered white bandages.

"What is it?" Bess asked.

Nancy jumped back. "It's, it's—a mummy!" she cried.

6

Down for the Count

M-m-maybe it's Sally!" Bess cried.

"Maybe Harriet did this to her for being so clumsy," George said.

"Let's get out of here!" Nancy said. But just as she was about to slam the locker door shut, the mummy tumbled out.

The girls shrieked as the mummy dropped on top of them. It was so heavy that they all fell to the ground in a heap.

"What's going on here?" came a voice.

Nancy peeked out from under the mummy's arm. She saw Sally, dressed in her Bride of Frankenstein costume.

Nancy pointed up at the mummy. "Um . . . this was in your locker," she said.

Sally dragged the mummy off the girls. "Whose joke was this?" she asked.

Suddenly a witch with a broom jumped out from behind a fake dead tree.

"Surprise!" the witch cackled. "I see you found your mummy!"

Bess hid behind Nancy.

"Who's that?" Nancy asked Sally.

Sally smiled. "That's my friend Maria, warts and all."

Maria turned to Sally.

"I stuck Mister Mummy in your locker right after you put on your costume," Maria explained. She shook her finger at Sally. "You always forget to lock your locker."

"I know." Sally groaned. "That's why I came back down here."

"*You* put the mummy in Sally's locker?" George asked Maria. "How come?"

"I thought Sally needed some cheering up," Maria said. She leaned on her broom. "Especially after yesterday's chocolate sundae disaster."

Nancy tapped the mummy. It sounded hollow. "This thing is fake, isn't it?"

Sally nodded. "It's made of papier-mâché. But it sure fooled you, huh?"

"Nah," George said. "Not me."

Bess turned to Maria. "If you wanted to cheer Sally up, why didn't you just give her flowers or chocolate?"

"Are you kidding?" Maria asked. She straightened her pointed hat. "Sally is allergic to chocolate."

"Really?" Nancy asked Sally.

Sally shuddered. "I wish I could eat chocolate-chip cookies, brownies, or chocolate ice cream, but when I do, I itch all over."

Then Sally folded her arms across her chest. "What were you girls doing in my locker anyway?" she asked.

Nancy took a deep breath. "We're trying to find out who baked the creepy cake that Harriet served yesterday," she explained.

Maria waved her black cape. "Don't look at me. I just mix brews."

"And I don't even touch chocolate," Sally said. Then she blushed. "Unless I drop a tray."

"Do you have any idea who might have baked the cake?" Nancy asked.

Sally shook her black-and-silver wig. "Not a clue. But good luck."

"Yeah, and when you find him, let me know," Maria said. She waved her broom. "I'll turn him into a toad. Cackle! Cackle!"

Nancy, Bess, and George giggled.

"Do you really think Sally is innocent, Nancy?" George asked as they climbed the stairs.

"Yes," Nancy said. "Why would anyone allergic to chocolate bake a chocolate cake?"

George grabbed Nancy's arm. "Now can we check out Count Snackula, pleeeease?"

"Okay, okay," Nancy said. She crossed Sally's name out of her notebook. Then they headed for Count Snackula's Castle.

When they got there, they saw a note pinned to the heavy black curtain. It read: Keep Out. This Means You!

"It's another joke," Nancy said.

The girls peeked through the heavy velvet curtain. The small room was empty.

"It looks even creepier when nobody's in there," George whispered.

Nancy saw cobwebs hanging from the ceiling. A coffin stood against one wall. Over the coffin was a fake owl on a perch. Its eyes glowed red.

"The sign says to keep out," Bess said in a tiny voice. "Are we sure we want to go inside?"

"Yes, we're sure," George hissed.

Nancy slipped through the heavy curtain. Bess and George followed.

"Let's look around for anything creepy," Nancy suggested.

"This whole place is creepy," Bess complained.

But then Nancy saw something that made her eyes open wide. On the lid of the coffin was a dab of white cream.

"Look at that," Nancy said. She pointed to the cream.

"Didn't the cake have whipped-cream squiggles on the top?" George asked.

Nancy nodded. "But how do we know that's whipped cream on the coffin? It could be shaving cream."

"And vampires must shave," Bess said. "They're not fuzzy like were-wolves."

"There's only one way to find out what it is," George said. "Someone has to taste it."

"Eeew," Bess said. "I'm not tasting that stuff."

"Neither am I," Nancy said.

Just then a rubber bat bounced down from the ceiling. Bess screamed and fell against the wall.

"Bess, watch out," Nancy said.

"You're leaning against some kind of switch!"

"What switch?" Bess asked.

But it was too late. The room began to fill up with thick, white fog.

"Great!" Nancy groaned as the fog drifted up past her knees. "Just great!"

7

Handle with Scare

Let's get out of here!" Nancy called through the fog.

"How?" Bess cried. "I can't see a thing!"

Nancy, Bess, and George fumbled through the thick mist for the way out.

"I think I found the curtain," Nancy said. She tugged at the heavy fabric.

"Good afternoon," came a voice.

Nancy jumped back. The fabric she'd grabbed wasn't the curtain. It was someone's cape.

Nancy, Bess, and George clutched one another as the fog began to thin.

When the room was finally clear, they were looking up into the angry face of Count Snackula.

"Didn't you girls read the sign?" Count Snackula asked.

Bess shrugged. "We thought that was just for . . . um . . . um . . ."

"Vampire slayers," George said quickly.

Nancy marched up to Count Snackula.

"We came in here for a reason," Nancy said bravely. "To look for clues."

"Nancy, don't," Bess whispered.

"Clues?" Count Snackula asked.

"Yesterday someone switched Harriet's chocolate cake with a creepy one," Nancy said.

Count Snackula raised his skinny eyebrows. "And you think it was me?" he asked.

"We overheard you saying something about a cake," Nancy said.

"And getting even with Harriet," George added.

Count Snackula threw back his head and laughed.

"He even laughs like a bat," George whispered to Nancy.

"You're right," Count Snackula said. "I *did* want revenge against Harriet."

He walked to the coffin. Then he pointed a long, skinny finger at the lid.

"And the revenge is inside there," Count Snackula said slowly.

Nancy could hear herself gulp.

"Don't you want to see what it is?" Count Snackula asked.

"No!" Bess said.

"Yes!" Nancy and George said.

"Then come," Count Snackula said.

Nancy, Bess, and George walked very slowly over to Count Snackula.

Count Snackula grabbed the lid and lifted it. It made a soft creaking sound.

"I've been *dying* to show this to someone," Count Snackula said.

Nancy held her breath as she peeked inside. "Ohmygosh!" she cried.

Inside the coffin was a cake. It was decorated with candy bats and whipped cream. Written on top in blue squiggles were the words: I QUIT!

"Does this take the cake, or what?" Count Snackula cried.

"This is your revenge?" Nancy asked.

"Oh, yes," the count said. "Now Harriet will have to find another Count Snackula."

Nancy watched as Count Snackula yanked his fangs from his mouth.

"No more candy bats for me!" he cried. "I'm opening up a flower shop!"

Count Snackula waved his cape in the air. Then he turned around and walked out.

Nancy, Bess, and George stared at the black curtain.

"He forgot his cake," Bess said.

"So that was the cake he was talking about," Nancy said.

"I guess that rules out Count Snackula," George said.

Bess turned to Nancy. "Then who?"

Suddenly the fake owl began to twist its head. Its red eyes flashed.

"Hoo!" it screeched.

The girls ran for the curtain. But as they spilled out of the room, they crashed right into Scott.

"Careful!" Scott cried as his baking tools tumbled out of his pocket.

"We're sorry," Nancy said. They kneeled down to help Scott pick them up.

But when Nancy grabbed a mixing spoon, she noticed something strange. There was green slime on the handle.

Scott snatched the spoon from Nancy. "I'll take that," he said quickly.

When all the tools were back in Scott's pocket, he stood up.

"Are you going back to the kitchen?" Nancy asked.

"No," Scott said. He walked away quickly. "I'm going to the basement for a bag of sugar."

Nancy watched Scott hurry away.

"Slime," Nancy said slowly.

"No, he's not," George said. "Scott's nice."

"I meant that there was green slime on one of his mixing spoons," Nancy explained.

Nancy opened her notebook and

added the slimy spoon to her list of clues.

"Do you think Scott might have baked the creepy cake?" George asked.

Nancy thought for a moment.

"Scott can bake," she said. "He's also in the kitchen all the time."

"And he seemed really nervous when he burned those muffins," Bess said.

George snapped her fingers. "Maybe there are some clues in Scott's cabinet."

Nancy nodded. "Let's check it out."

"But he'll see us!" Bess cried.

"Scott just went down to the basement," Nancy said. "And I saw Harriet talking to some diners. If we hurry, we can get into the kitchen while it's still empty."

The three friends rushed through the dining area to the dessert kitchen. Nancy was right. It *was* empty.

"Open Scott's cabinet, Nancy," Bess said.

Nancy grabbed the handle on the

cabinet door. Then she pulled it open and looked in.

The cabinet was stocked with jars and bottles of baking ingredients. Nancy read the labels out loud: "Corn syrup, oil, vanilla extract . . ."

George reached in. She moved some jars aside. "What's that bottle in the back? The one without a label?"

Nancy carefully took the brown bottle from the cabinet.

"I know," she said. "This is the same bottle that the mad scientist showed us."

"You mean the one with the slime?" Bess said.

"Are you sure?" George asked. She grabbed the bottle from Nancy's hand.

"Don't open it, George!" Nancy cried.

But it was too late. George had already popped the cap off the bottle. Green slime oozed from the top. It bubbled down George's hand and all over the kitchen floor.

"Oh, no!" Nancy cried.

8

Scene of the Slime

I t's out of control!" George shouted.

"Ugh!" Bess shrieked. "It's all over my new shoes!"

Nancy didn't know what to do. She grabbed a bucket and dropped it over the oozing bottle. The green slime seeped out from under it.

"The mad scientist was right," George said. "That stuff *is* alive!"

Just then the door swung open and Harriet ran in. "What's all this green slime doing in my kitchen?" she asked.

Bess and George froze like statues. Nancy took a deep breath. Then she explained everything to Harriet.

"You think Scott baked that horrible cake?" Harriet asked Nancy.

"I didn't!" came an angry voice.

Nancy spun around. It was Scott.

"That green stuff you saw on my spoon was . . . from a key lime pie I was baking."

Nancy pointed to the floor. "You mean a key *slime* pie."

"Where did you find that?" Scott asked.

"In your cabinet," George said. "Right next to the marshmallow topping."

Scott looked angry. He stepped carefully over the green gook. Then he reached to close his cabinet.

"That's ridiculous," Scott said. "Why would I keep slime in my—"

"Look out!" George called.

A paper bag inside the cabinet tipped over. It spilled fake eyeballs all over Scott.

"Arrrrgh!" Scott shouted as the eyeballs rolled off his shoulders.

Harriet folded her arms across her

chest. "Green slime? Fake eyeballs? I think you have some explaining to do, Scott Martin," she said.

"Okay, okay," Scott said. He kicked a plastic eyeball away from his foot. "I did bake the creepy cake."

Bess grabbed Nancy's arm excitedly.

"But it wasn't for Tory," he said. "It was for my little cousin, Ryan."

"Your cousin?" Bess asked. "Why did you bake him such a gross cake?"

"Ryan loves anything gross," Scott explained. "So I collected rubber spiders, green slime, fake eyeballs, and anything else I could find here in the restaurant."

"But how did all that stuff land up with Tory?" Nancy asked.

"I baked the cake in my free time. After I filled it, I placed it next to the others," Scott said. "I had no idea you would choose it as Tory's birthday cake."

"Why didn't you just admit it yesterday, Scott?" Harriet asked.

"I didn't want you to know that I was

goofing around in the kitchen," Scott said.

"I *am* mad that you baked this cake behind my back, Scott," Harriet said.

Then Nancy saw Harriet smile.

"But it seems like a trick *I* would have played in college," Harriet said.

"Nancy's aunt Eloise told us all about those tricks, Harriet," George said. "They must have been fun."

"Tricks can be fun," Harriet said. "But they can sometimes backfire."

"Like yesterday," Scott said slowly. "When I ruined your review."

Just then Nancy had an idea.

"I know!" she said. "Let's go to Tory's apartment and explain what happened with the cake."

"You mean everything?" Scott asked.

Nancy nodded. "As my dad always says, there's nothing better than telling the truth."

"Good idea, Nancy," Harriet said. "I'll call Mrs. Buckingham to ask if you can come over."

After a quick lunch at Haunted Harriet's, Scott took the girls to Tory's building. It was only a few blocks from the restaurant.

"Scott?" Nancy asked as they entered the building. "Did you also write that slimy message on the mirror yesterday?"

"What slimy message?" Scott asked.

Nancy sighed. "Never mind."

As they walked through the lobby, Bess gasped. "This place looks like a castle!"

A man behind a desk phoned up to Tory's apartment. Then he smiled.

"You can take the elevator up to Apartment Twenty S," he said.

George snickered. *"S* as in *snooty,"*

"Shhh!" Nancy said.

They rang the doorbell, and Mrs. Buckingham answered the door. "Tory is in her room," she said coolly. "Why don't you come with me?"

They followed Mrs. Buckingham to a large room filled with toys and games. Tory was sitting on her bed with her arms folded across her chest.

"I don't want to listen to them," Tory said with a pout. "I just want to play with my new birthday presents."

"But we came to explain what happened with the gross cake," Nancy said.

"Don't remind me about that stupid cake," Tory cried. "I had to wash my hair three times!"

"Tory, dear," Mrs. Buckingham said. "Let's hear what they have to say."

Then Mrs. Buckingham turned to Scott. "And it had better be good!" she growled.

Scott explained everything that had happened. When he was finished, Mrs. Buckingham and Tory didn't say a word.

Uh-oh, Nancy thought. They're going to start yelling any minute.

But suddenly Tory began to laugh. "You mean all that gross stuff was supposed to be for your cousin?" she asked.

Mrs. Buckingham began to laugh, too. "What a mix-up!" she cried.

"You're not mad?" Nancy asked.

"I was pretty mad yesterday," Tory said. "But later on the cake reminded me of my favorite TV show, *Slime Time*."

"You mean where kids have to swim though slime to win prizes?" George asked.

"That's a great show," Nancy said.

Mrs. Buckingham shook Scott's hand. "Apology accepted, Scott," she said.

Tory walked over to Nancy. "I'd like to apologize, too," she said. "I wrote that mean message on the mirror. I did it when my hands were covered with slime."

Nancy smiled. So it was Tory who had written the message. Now the mystery was really solved.

"That's okay," Nancy said. "You must have been pretty angry."

Then Tory walked over to her toy shelf and reached for the Statue of Liberty doll.

"Why don't you take this?" Tory

69

asked. "I got plenty of new stuff on my birthday."

Nancy took the Statue of Liberty doll and held it carefully. "Thanks, Tory."

"I'd like to make an offer, too," Mrs. Buckingham said. "How would you like me to come back to Haunted Harriet's tomorrow to write a new review for my magazine?"

"Harriet would love it," Scott said.

"Would you girls like to join us there?" Mrs. Buckingham asked.

Nancy shook her head. "Thank you, but we have to go home to River Heights tomorrow morning," she said.

"Well, then," Mrs. Buckingham said. "How about a horse and carriage ride right now?"

"A horse and carriage ride?" Bess squealed.

"Cool!" George cried.

"We'd love it!" Nancy said.

"Thanks, but I can't go," Scott said. "I have to get back to work."

Mrs. Buckingham turned to Nancy. "Do you know someone else who would like to join you, Nancy?" she asked.

"I sure do," Nancy said. "That is, if she's finished grading math tests."

The sun was just going down as a beautiful horse and white carriage made its way down Fifth Avenue.

"Look at all the stores!" Bess cried.

"And all the people!" George said.

Aunt Eloise smiled at Nancy. "So, Nancy. What do you think of your trip to New York City?"

"It's awesome," Nancy said. "But there's just one thing I have to do."

"What?" Tory asked. "See Times Square? The United Nations? Radio City Music Hall?"

"No, this," Nancy said. She took out her detective notebook and opened it in her lap. Then she began to write:

When it comes to cases, this one took the cake—the *creepy* cake! But I learned a lot. First, that practical jokes sometimes aren't very funny. So you

have to be real careful. Second, I learned something about myself: If I can solve a mystery in a big city like New York, then I guess I can solve one just about anywhere!

Case closed.

**Do your younger brothers and sisters
want to read books like yours?**

**Let them know there
are books just for *them*!**

They can join Nancy Drew and her best
friends as they collect clues and solve
mysteries in

THE NANCY DREW NOTEBOOKS®

Starting with

#1 The Slumber Party Secret

#2 The Lost Locket

#3 The Secret Santa

#4 Bad Day for Ballet

**AND
Meet up with suspense and mystery
in Frank and Joe Hardy:
The Clues Brothers™**

Starting with

#1 The Gross Ghost Mystery

#2 The Karate Clue

#3 First Day, Worst Day

#4 Jump Shot Detectives

Look for a brand-new story every
other month at your local bookseller